FAVOURITE TALES

The Ugly Duckling

illustrated
by
PETULA STONE

based on the story by Hans Christian Andersen

It was summer in the country. All the hay had been stacked, and the fields of wheat were yellow. Tall dock leaves grew on the banks of the canals.

Among the dock leaves, on her nest, sat a duck waiting for her eggs to hatch. She had been waiting for a long time.

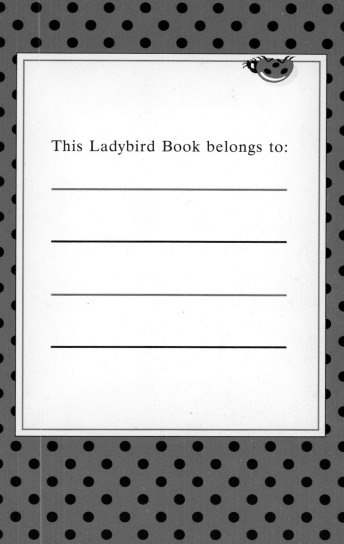

This Ladybird Book belongs to:

_____

_____

_____

_____

This Ladybird retelling
by
Lynne Bradbury

Published by Ladybird Books Ltd
27 Wrights Lane London W8 5TZ
A Penguin Company
5 7 9 10 8 6 4

Printed in Italy

At last the eggs began to crack and,
one by one, the ducklings
poked their heads out.

Before long, all the eggs had hatched except the biggest one. The duck sat a little longer, until out tumbled the last of her chicks.

But when she looked at him, she said, "Oh, dear! You're so big and ugly."

The next day was warm and sunny, so the duck took her new family down to the canal. She splashed into the water and, one by one, her ducklings followed her. Soon all of them were swimming beautifully, even the ugly grey one.

Next the ducklings went into the duck yard. "Stay close to me," warned their mother. The other ducks thought the ducklings were beautiful – all except the big ugly one.

The ducklings stayed in the duck yard.
But the ugly duckling was very unhappy
there. The older ducks pecked at him
and laughed. He had nowhere to hide,
so one day he ran away.

He ran and ran until he came to the great marsh where the wild ducks lived. There he lay in the rushes for two whole weeks.

Then some wild ducks and some geese came to look at him. "You're *very* ugly," they said, and they laughed at him.

The poor little ugly duckling ran away
from the great marsh. He ran and ran
over fields and meadows. The wind
blew and the rain rained. The
duckling was cold, wet and very tired.

Just as it was getting dark, the
duckling found a little cottage.

The cottage was very old and the door was falling off. This left a gap just big enough for the duckling to creep inside, out of the cold.

An old woman lived there. She had a cat that purred and a hen that laid eggs. She found the cold, starving little duckling in the morning.

The old woman looked at the
duckling and said, "You can stay.
Now we shall have duck eggs
to eat, too!"

So the duckling stayed. But he *didn't*
lay eggs.

The cat said to him, "Can you purr?"

"No," said the duckling.

The hen asked, "Can you lay eggs?"

"No," said the duckling, sadly.

"Then you must go,"
said the cat and
the hen.

So the ugly duckling was alone once again. He walked in the marshes and floated on the water, and everywhere he went, all the birds and animals said, "How big and *ugly* you are."

Winter was coming. The leaves began to fall from the trees, and the ground was cold and hard.

The duckling had nowhere to stay.

One evening a flock of birds flew overhead. They were beautiful white swans with long necks.

"I wish *I* was like that," the duckling said sadly to himself.

He travelled on and on and the winter grew colder.

The ground froze and the duckling couldn't find food. One night, as he was pecking to find water, he was so tired that he fell asleep on the ice.

The next morning a farmer found the duckling and took him home so that his wife could take care of him.

As the duckling grew stronger, the
farmer's children wanted to play with
him. But the children were rough, and
the duckling was frightened when
they chased him. As soon as he could,
he ran away again.

At last the duckling found a safe
hiding place among the reeds in the
marsh. There he stayed for the rest of
the winter.

Then, after many long weeks, the
warm spring sun began to shine again.
The duckling spread his wings – they
were strong wings now. Suddenly he
rose from the ground and flew high
into the air.

Down below, three beautiful swans were swimming on the canal. The duckling flew down to look at them. As he landed, the lonely bird saw his own reflection in the water.

He wasn't an ugly duckling at all! During the long winter he had grown into a beautiful white swan.

The other swans looked at him and admired his grace and beauty. "Come with us," they said.

And he did!

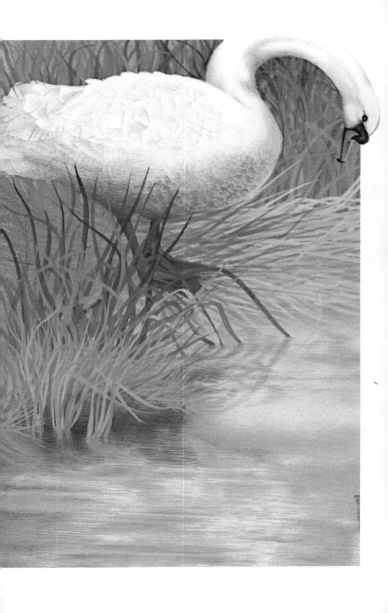